About This Book

Title: *I Can Do It!*

Step: 2

Word Count: 118

Skills in Focus: Consonant Blends: Initial and Final (dr-, pr-, sl-, sn-, sp-, -lf, -nd, -nk, -st)

Tricky Words: by, do, keep, me, my, myself, rinse

Ideas for Using this Book

Before Reading:
- **Comprehension**: Read the title. Talk about what the boy is doing on the cover of the story. Look through the pictures in the story. What else is the little boy doing? Do you do activities like this at home?
- **Accuracy**: Practice the tricky words listed on Page 1.
- **Phonemic Awareness**: Explain that the readers will read words with the *sp-* blend. A blend is two or more consonants together that each make a sound. Practice taking apart and putting together the sounds in *spot*: Say the word *spot*. Move counters or any other object forward as you say each sound. How many sounds are in the word *spot*? What is the first sound? Second sound? Third sound? End sound? Repeat with other *sp-* story words: spell, spit, spill.

During Reading:
- Have the reader point under each word as they read it.
- **Decoding**: Point out any words in the story that have a blend. If stuck on a word, help them say each sound and blend it together smoothly.
- **Comprehension**: As you read about all the things the character can do, invite students to make connections to what they can do. Ask them about how they lend a hand or what they do to get ready for school in the morning.

After Reading:
Discuss the book. Some ideas for questions:
- Who is Spot?
- What are some of the things the narrator, or the person telling the story, can do by himself at home? At school?
- What are some things you can do by yourself at home or at school?

I Can Do It!

Text by Leanna Koch
Educational content by Kristen Cowen

Illustrated by
Shirley Beckes

PICTURE WINDOW BOOKS
a capstone imprint

Spot is fond of me. I am fond of Spot. Spot and I can get up.

I can do it, Spot.
I can dress myself.

I can prep my bed for rest.

I can pack up.

I can lend a hand.

I can spell. I will do my best on the test.

I can keep my hands snug.

I can pick up my sled.
If I slip, I will get up.

I can keep my jacket on this rack.

I can tend my tank.

I can set this all up. If I spill it, I can pick it up.

I can rinse and spit.

I can pick up this stuff.

I can rest. I can do a lot!

More Ideas:

Phonemic Awareness Activity

Practicing Initial and Final Blends:
Provide the reader with a small pile of beads or other small tokens. For each word, say it to the reader and have them slowly stretch out the sounds, moving one bead as they say each sound. Reinforce the blend being in the initial or final position.

Optional: Draw four boxes (Elkonin boxes) to move each bead into.

- h-a-n-d
- s-p-a-n
- t-a-n-k
- s-l-i-p
- s-n-u-g

Extended Learning Activity

I Am Responsible:
The child in the story demonstrates responsibility by completing many tasks at home and school independently! What are some tasks you can do on your own? Make a list of tasks together. Draw a line down the middle of a blank piece of paper and have the students illustrate a task they perform at home and at school.

Optional: Provide a sentence starter for the student to write about each picture. (I can _____ at home/school.)

Published by Picture Window Books,
an imprint of Capstone
1710 Roe Crest Drive,
North Mankato, Minnesota 56003
capstonepub.com

I Can Do It! was originally published as
I Am in Charge of Me, copyright 2004 by Picture Window Books.

Copyright© 2024 by Capstone.
All rights reserved. No part of this publication may be reproduced
in whole or in part, or stored in a retrieval system, or transmitted in
any form or by any means, electronic, mechanical, photocopying,
recording, or otherwise, without written permission of the publisher.

Library of Congress Cataloging-in-Publication Data is available
on the Library of Congress website.

ISBN: 9780756595135 (hardback)
ISBN: 9780756583897 (paperback)
ISBN: 9780756583873 (eBook PDF)

Printed and bound in the USA. 5757